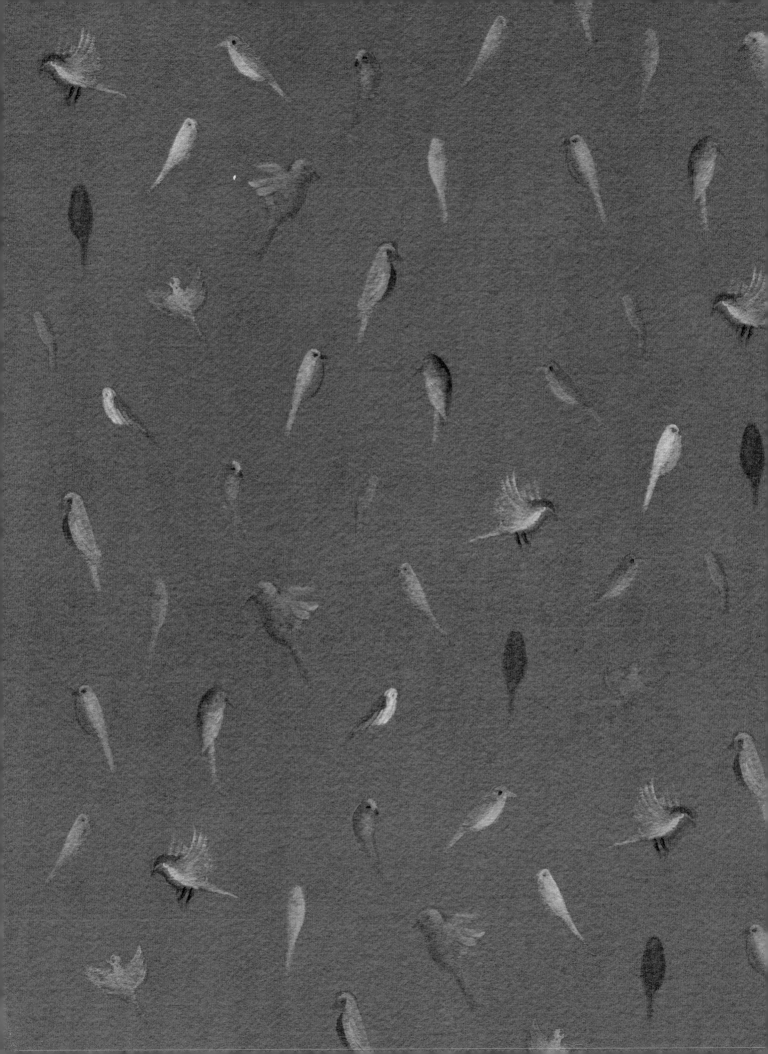

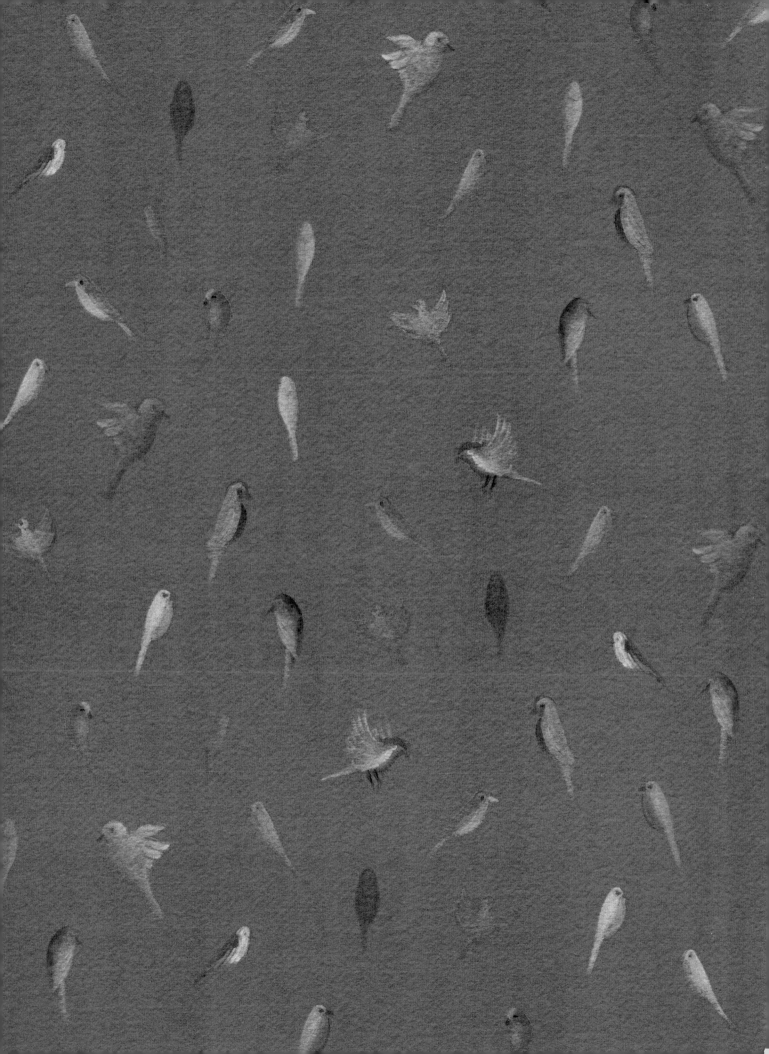

For Nefeterius, Mom, Noah, Milo, Zen, Lotus, Charles
and the baby bird on Via del Babuino

www.theenglishschoolhouse.com

Text copyright © 2018 by Tamara Pizzoli
Pictures copyright © 2018 by Elena Tommasi Ferroni
All rights reserved.

ISBN: 978-0-9976860-1-2

LOTUS AND THE BABY BIRD

Dr. Tamara Pizzoli

Illustrated by Elena Tommasi Ferroni

THE ENGLISH SCHOOL HOUSE

Lotus had lived on Via del Babuino in Rome, Italy
her whole life – a total of eight years.

She knew everyone there was to know in the area: Iris the
baker, Federico the sandwich shop owner, Paola the woman who
ran the jewelry store right underneath her home, and so many
others. They had all seen Lotus grow and evolve from an infant
into a spunky kid with a few permanent teeth.

As Lotus grew, so did her hair, and she preferred to wear it just as it sprouted from her scalp… glorious.

Naturally, her hair garnered a significant amount of attention
from both strangers and those who knew Lotus best.

"Mamma mia! Che capelli!"

"What hair!" strangers would exclaim as she rode her scooter
around Piazza del Popolo after school.

Others offered unsolicited wise cracks poorly delivered as jokes.
"What, did someone scare you today?" a stranger would quip.
"Did you put your finger in the electrical socket
 and get shocked?" another would grin and chuckle.

Lotus's mother, however, had long before taught her the perfect response to such unsavory remarks.

"Tell them the truth every time they ask, " she'd instructed Lotus when she began la scuola materna, or preschool, around age three.

"When they ask you about your hair, tell them it is your crown." She continued, "And you, princess, are never required to let anyone touch your crown."

And that's precisely what Lotus told anyone who inquired about her coils, each and every time.

After pre-school, Lotus began her elementary school education at la scuola San Giuseppe, St. Joseph school, in Piazza di Spagna. Now that she was eight years old and San Giuseppe was near their home, her parents permitted her to walk to and from school on her own each morning and afternoon.

One Tuesday morning Lotus was strolling on the sidewalk on her way to class when something plunged from the sky above, just barely missing her nose, and landed with a thud on the concrete right before her two feet. Curious, Lotus bent down to examine what had fallen, and her heart sank when she observed a seemingly lifeless baby bird that, she assumed, had plummeted from its warm nest straight to its death on the ground below.

Shaken and saddened, and for reasons she'd later spend countless moments trying to comprehend, Lotus continued walking and left the baby bird motionless in the middle of the sidewalk. By the time she reached Piazza di Spagna, an intense urge to help, or at least move the baby bird, overcame her. She pivoted and returned to the exact spot where she'd last seen the tiny creature.

Only when she arrived, nothing but remnants of the baby bird remained. Someone had stepped on it as they walked to their destination, crushing it beyond recognition.

Lotus's heart sank. An attempt to describe the disappointment and guilt that swelled in her heart would be difficult indeed. Lotus was so overcome with melancholy and regret that she could hardly think or speak of anything else at school that day.

She had let the baby bird down, she felt.
And the questions and wonderings that now consumed her thoughts were seemingly endless:
What if the baby bird hadn't died instantly?
What if it had suffered?
What if it was only too injured to move after such a great fall?
Why hadn't she acted sooner?
Why hadn't she done something to help immediately?
If she would have arrived just two seconds earlier, she mused, the baby bird would have landed safely in a warm, welcome nest of sorts – in her crown.

That night, as her mother helped her wash her hair in the bathtub, Lotus explained every detail of what had occurred. Her mother listened with great attention, then smiled and stroked her daughter's forehead.

Lotus expressed how she wished she'd at least moved the baby bird right away or, even better, that she'd made sure it was no longer breathing instead of just assuming... or that she'd gotten there just two seconds earlier so that the baby bird would have landed safely in her curls instead of the unforgiving concrete.

Her mother nodded and smiled gently, then spoke.
"Lotus, my love, it is fine that you feel pain about what happened to the baby bird, but you mustn't blame yourself. That will only cause you to suffer. Things went as they were meant to go. And the baby bird taught you a lesson, am I right? You still love the bird, even if it is no longer living. Love transcends time and circumstance. Here's the thing, sweetheart – focusing on what should have, could have, or would have happened won't change a thing. You see, you can't change the past, but once you know better, you can do better. Your job is to use what you've learned. You can't change the past, but the future is all yours to create."

Lotus nodded, and she decided that
she'd learn and know all she could.

And that's exactly what she did.

"It's my crown."

The wound is the place where the light enters you.
–Rumi

Dear Reader,

The illustrations for this story were created by master Italian
painter Elena Tommasi Ferroni in Rome, Italy. She used oil on
paper to produce visual jewels to interpret this story. Some of
the original paintings and prints of all of the art in this work are
available for purchase at www.theenglishschoolhouse.com
as well as through The Nef Gallery, www.thenefgallery.com.

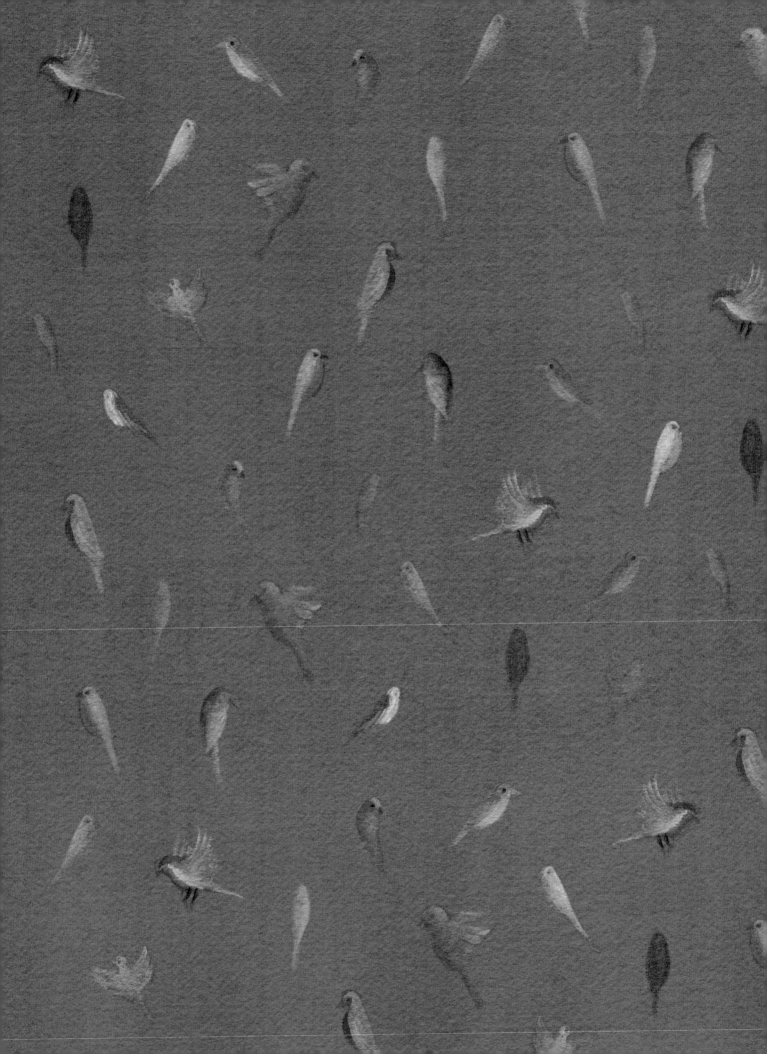

Made in the USA
Columbia, SC
29 June 2019